What would Evelyn Margaret Think, Say, and Do?

tate publishing
CHILDREN'S DIVISION

SO-ADZ-068

Christina K. Hanrahan

Published by Tate Publishing & Enterprises, LLC
127 E. Trade Center Terrace | Mustang, Oklahoma 73064 USA
1.888.361.9473 | www.tatepublishing.com

Tate Publishing is committed to excellence in the publishing industry. The company reflects the philosophy established by the founders, based on Psalm 68:11,
"The Lord gave the word and great was the company of those who published it."

Book design copyright © 2013 by Tate Publishing, LLC. All rights reserved.
Cover and interior design by Alexis Dominique C. Limpiado
Illustrations by Noelle Barcelo

Published in the United States of America
ISBN: 9781625103895
1. Juvenile Fiction / Girls & Women)
2. Juvenile Fiction / Health & Daily Living / Daily Activities
13.06.06

Dedication

To my uncles, Leon and Richard,
Susan, her mother Carol, Molly,
Jerrica, and Lisa C. to whom without,
this book simply would not be.

What Would Evelyn Margaret Think?

What would Evelyn Margaret think if all she had to wear was pink?

What would Evelyn Margaret think if she dropped her key down the kitchen sink?

What would Evelyn Margaret think if she missed her ride to the skating rink?

I'll tell you what Evelyn Margaret would think. She would think pink is a pretty nice color to wear to the rink.

As for dropping her key down the kitchen sink, she would ask her favorite uncles, who would get it out with a smile, a twist, and a clink.

And as for missing her ride to the skating rink, she would politely ask her best friend Molly Sue's mommy, who she just knew would help her in a blink. That is what Evelyn Margaret would think.

What Would Evelyn Margaret Say?

What would Evelyn Margaret say if she were having a really bad day?

What would Evelyn Margaret say if she could not find her purple beret?

What would Evelyn Margaret say if she could not go to the park to play?

I'll tell you what Evelyn Margaret would say. She would say, "This day will get better if I just sit down and pray."

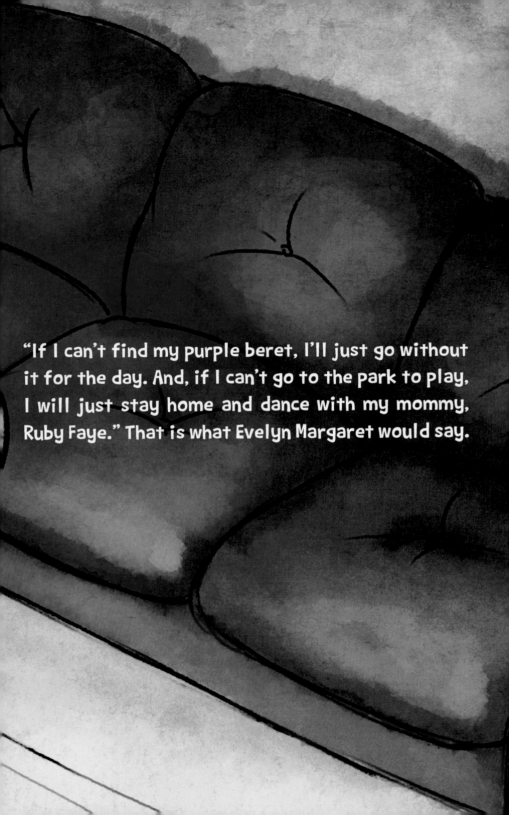

"If I can't find my purple beret, I'll just go without it for the day. And, if I can't go to the park to play, I will just stay home and dance with my mommy, Ruby Faye." That is what Evelyn Margaret would say.

What Would Evelyn Margaret Do?

What would Evelyn Margaret do if she were unable to tie her shoe?

What would Evelyn Margaret do if it were too cold to go to the zoo?

What would Evelyn Margaret do if she could not play with her best friend, Molly Sue?

I'll tell you what Evelyn Margaret would do. She would ask her mommy to help her tie her shoe and then keep practicing until she could tie it too.

She would stay warm inside imagining herself at the zoo and draw pictures of her favorite animals, the buffalo and the caribou.

And, since she could not play with her best friend, Molly Sue, she would call her on the telephone and tell her not to be blue. That is what Evelyn Margaret would do.

e|LIVE

---

listen|imagine|view|experience

AUDIO BOOK DOWNLOAD INCLUDED WITH THIS BOOK!

In your hands you hold a complete digital entertainment package. In addition to the paper version, you receive a free download of the audio version of this book. Simply use the code listed below when visiting our website. Once downloaded to your computer, you can listen to the book through your computer's speakers, burn it to an audio CD or save the file to your portable music device (such as Apple's popular iPod) and listen on the go!

How to get your free audio book digital download:

1. Visit www.tatepublishing.com and click on the e|LIVE logo on the home page.
2. Enter the following coupon code:
   76dd-d458-a8c1-4fee-b5ba-3891-22b6-7307
3. Download the audio book from your e|LIVE digital locker and begin enjoying your new digital entertainment package today!